Samuel French Acting Edition

I0591736

Gunmetal Blues

A Musical Mystery

Book by
Scott Wentworth

Music and Lyrics by
Craig Bohmler & Marion Adler

*The character of Buddy Toupee was
inspired by the work of Richard March*

SAMUELFRENCH.COM   SAMUELFRENCH.CO.UK

www.SamuelFrench.com
www.SamuelFrench.co.uk

FOR PRODUCTION ENQUIRIES

UNITED STATES AND CANADA
Info@SamuelFrench.com
1-866-598-8449

UNITED KINGDOM AND EUROPE
Plays@SamuelFrench.co.uk
020-7255-4302

Each title is subject to availability from Samuel French, depending upon country of performance. Please be aware that *GUNMETAL BLUES* may not be licensed by Samuel French in your territory. Professional and amateur producers should contact the nearest Samuel French office or licensing partner to verify availability.

MUSIC USE NOTE

Licensees are solely responsible for obtaining formal written permission from copyright owners to use copyrighted music in the performance of this play and are strongly cautioned to do so. If no such permission is obtained by the licensee, then the licensee must use only original music that the licensee owns and controls. Licensees are solely responsible and liable for all music clearances and shall indemnify the copyright owners of the play(s) and their licensing agent, Samuel French, against any costs, expenses, losses and liabilities arising from the use of music by licensees. Please contact the appropriate music licensing authority in your territory for the rights to any incidental music.

IMPORTANT BILLING AND CREDIT REQUIREMENTS

If you have obtained performance rights to this title, please refer to your licensing agreement for important billing and credit requirements.

The following credits must be included in all programs, advertising, and otherwise publicizing or expiating a production of the play:

Gunmetal Blues was partially developed and received readings during the 1989 National Music Theatre Conference at the O'Neill Theatre Center, with the support of the Lila Wallace Reader's Digest Fund.

GUNMETAL BLUES is dedicated in loving memory to Richard March.

Gunmetal Blues premiered on May 30, 1991 at the Phoenix Little Theatre in association with the Musical Theatre of Arizona. It was directed by Michael Barnard and had the following cast:

THE PIANO PLAYER.................Jerry Wayne Harkey
THE BLONDE....................................Heidi Ewart
THE PRIVATE EYE ....Robert D. Mammana

Musical Direction: Jerry Wayne Harkey
Set Design: Tom Oldendick
Lighting Design: Ron Newcomer
Costume Design: Rebecca Powell
Makeup and Hair Design: Barbara "B.J." Hart

Gunmetal Blues was first professionally produced by Theatre New Brunswick. It was directed by Glynis Leyshon.

THE PIANO PLAYER........................ Doug Balfour
THE BLONDE.................................Marion Adler
THE PRIVATE EYE .... James Carroll

Musical Director: Craig Bohmler
Set & Costume Design: Charlotte Dean
Lighting Designer: Luc Prairie
Stage Manager: Jill Beatty
Assistant Stage Manager: Judith Begley

Gunmetal Blues was subsequently presented Off-Broadway in New York by the Amas Musical Theatre, Inc., Rosetta LeNoire, Artistic Director, William Michael Maher, Producing Director.

THE PIANO PLAYER...................... Daniel Marcus
THE BLONDE ....Marion Adler
THE PRIVATE EYE .... Scott Wentworth
THE BARKEEP ....Michael Knowles
MUSICIANS:
    Sax, Clarinet & Flute............................Steve Hull
    Bass ....Marcus Lauper
    Percussion .... David Cossin

Directed by: Davis Hall
Scenery & Costumes Designed by: Eduardo Sicangco
Lighting Designed by: Scott Zielinski
Musical Direction: Craig Bohmler
Production Stage Manager: Lisa Ledwich
Production Manager: J. Greg De Felice

Authors' Notes

GUNMETAL BLUES can be played in any number of theatrical settings from full-scale production (complete with set, costumes, three-piece band and even the addition of the non-speaking role of "the Barkeep") to cabaret-style (with only the three actors, a piano and a couple of stools). If a set is to be used, directors and designers should note that the entire play takes place in the Red Eye Lounge. All locations within the story (Sam's office, Wasp Tower, Mansion Hill, etc.) should be created in the audience's imagination through the use of lighting and staging. There are no scene changes.

As to the "look" of the show; although the action takes place in the present day, it should also be evocative of the late forties/early fifties. The men's costumes are pretty classic. Sam wears a suit, trenchcoat and fedora. Buddy wears a tux. The Blonde's costumes can be as emblematic or as fully realized as the production warrants, but they must be extremely practical in regard to the many quick changes the role requires.

A word about performance style; it is important that the play not be "sent up" or stylized to the point of camp. The humor comes, not from parody, but from the individual character's wit and sense of irony. The acting should be straightforward, clean and on the line.

MUSICAL NUMBERS

ACT I

"Welcome To This Window"............................ Buddy
"Don't Know What I Expected"..........Buddy/Sam/Laura
"Facts!"...Sam
"Loose Change"..................................... Princess
"Mansion Hill" .... Sam/Buddy
"Shadowplay" .... Buddy/Sam
"Skeletons" ....Laura
"The Blonde Song" ....Carol
"Childhood Days" .... Buddy/Sam/Carol
"Take A Break" .... Buddy

ACT II

"Buddy Toupee—Live"............................... Buddy
"Gunmetal Blues"... Sam
"I'm the One That Got Away"...................... Princess
"Jenny".. Sam
"Don't Know What I Expected" (Reprise)
.... Buddy/Sam/Carol
"Put It On My Tab" ....Carol
"The Virtuoso" .... Buddy
"Finale"...................................Buddy/Sam/Jenny

CHARACTERS

THE PIANO PLAYER

THE BLONDE

THE PRIVATE EYE

TIME & PLACE

The action takes place at the Red Eye Lounge. It's one of those bars in one of those hotels out by an airport.

Time: Tonight. Pretty late.

ACT I

DARKNESS. Maybe the sound of a PLANE taking off.
Then a melancholy TUNE is heard. [Music Cue #1:
BUDDY'S PRELUDE] The LIGHTS come up on a
piano player. This is BUDDY TOUPEE. After a while,
he speaks to the audience.

BUDDY.
Kinda quiet here tonight on the airport strip,
There's fog out on the runway and the moon is just a slip,
So why not stick around—I got another set to play,
It's (*Whatever day it really is*). night at the Red Eye
   Lounge ...
Hi, I'm Buddy Toupee.

[Music Cue #2: WELCOME TO THIS WINDOW]

WELCOME TO THIS WINDOW
PRESS YOUR CHEEK AGAINST THE PANE
CLEAR A CIRCLE ON THE GLASS
WHERE TEARS LEAVE STREAKS LIKE RAIN
SOMETHING HERE FOR EVERYONE
HOWEVER YOU'RE INCLINED
COME AND GET AN EYEFUL
BEFORE I PULL DOWN THE BLIND

(As BUDDY sings, a mysterious BLONDE enters,
   carrying a suitcase. SHE sits at a table.)

BON VOYAGE, MON VOYEUR
IT'S A JOURNEY OF PEEPING
WHERE SECRETS LIE NAKED
AND MYSTERIES LIE SLEEPING
I'LL SHOW YOU THEIR DREAMS

AS THEY TOSS IN THE NIGHT
IF YOU SEE A REFLECTION
IT'S JUST A TRICK OF LIGHT

*(As BUDDY continues, a private eye enters. HE sits at a
table. HE doesn't see the blonde. This is SAM
GALAHAD.)*

BUDDY.
WELCOME TO THIS WINDOW
THINK I'VE SEEN YOU HERE BEFORE
YOU MIGHT HAVE MISSED A CLUE
SO YOU KEEP COMING BACK FOR MORE
THE WORDS YOU DIDN'T SAY
THE HAND YOU WOULDN'T TOUCH
THE TRUTH YOU COULDN'T SEE
TILL YOU FINALLY SAW TOO MUCH

BON VOYAGE, MON VOYEUR
ON YOUR JOURNEY TO CAPTURE
THE LAWLESS IN CRIME
THE FAITHLESS IN RAPTURE
YOU WATCH AND YOU WAIT
WHAT YOU SEE NO ONE KNOWS
YOUR HEART NEVER OPENS
YOUR EYES NEVER CLOSE

SO WELCOME TO THIS WINDOW
WITH THE GLASS AGAINST YOUR SKIN
DOES IT REALLY MATTER IF YOU'RE LOOKING
   OUT OR IN
IT'S STILL THE SAME OLD STORY
I WOULDN'T STEER YOU WRONG
BUT BUDDY SERVES IT WITH A TWIST
SO WHY NOT COME ALONG?

BON VOYAGE, MON VOYEUR
ISN'T PEEPING A TRIP

WHEN WE MEET INCOGNITO
OUT HERE ON THE STRIP?
IT'S OUR LITTLE SECRET
OUR LITTLE MENAGE
SO WELCOME TO THIS WINDOW
(*Spoken.*) Mon Voyeur ...
BON VOYAGE

(The BLONDE exits as BUDDY plays. SAM turns in time to see the door swing shut. Maybe he catches a glimpse of her shadow. BUDDY plays the final chord. After the number, HE begins a slow "bluesy" vamp. [Music Cue #2A: GUNMETAL BLUES VAMP] SAM lights a cigarette.)

BUDDY. Don't look now,
He's right behind you,
He's the eyes in the match-light,
The hat in the rear-view mirror,
He's the face in the window,
But mostly—he's invisible,
He's Sam Galahad ...
He's your shadow.

(The LIGHTS have changed. SAM is looking out a window. BUDDY watches.)

SAM. It was one of those gray days in the city. Gray rain out of a gray sky. I was waiting for a client. A woman from Wasp Enterprises. I should have known it was going to be trouble. In this town, you couldn't spit without hitting something that had Adrian Wasp's name on it. On Mansion Hill they called him "the King."
BUDDY. They called him a lot of other things, too.
SAM. But he didn't care what they called him.
BUDDY. (*Stops playing.*) No?
SAM. Not since he put that bullet through his head.

(*SAM opens up a newspaper. The banner headline reads, "SUICIDE ON MANSION HILL!!!"*)

BUDDY. Oh. (*HE starts playing again, a new vamp—faster, like a walking bass. [Music Cue #3: DON'T KNOW WHAT I EXPECTED]*)

SAM. Then I heard the unmistakable tapping of expensive shoes on cheap linoleum.

(*The BLONDE enters, wearing dark glasses, a woman's fedora and a belted, form-fitting raincoat. This is LAURA VESPER.*)

BUDDY.
SHE WAS A PALE BLONDE WITH RICE PAPER SKIN
HER CHEEKBONES WERE HIGH AND HER LIPS WERE THIN
BEHIND THE SHADES HER EYES PLAYED A KINDA ROULETTE
SHE WAS BACK-LIT IN THE DOORWAY
SAM CHECKED HER SILHOUETTE
SHE SAID ...
    LAURA. Mr. Galahad?
    SAM. Last time I looked.
    LAURA. Sam Galahad? The private detective?
    SAM. That's what it says on the door.
    LAURA. Actually, it says "Rudy's Plumbing and Heating."
    SAM. The card must have fallen off. Please come in.
    BUDDY.
HIGH HEELS DID A TAP BREAK ON THE GRIMY TILE
SHE DIDN'T TAKE HER GLASSES OFF
SHE DIDN'T TRY TO SMILE
SHE CROSSED HER LEGS AND WAITED
SAM GAVE HER A STARE
SMOKE WAS A QUESTION MARK

HANGING IN THE AIR
LAURA.
DON'T KNOW WHAT I EXPECTED
BUDDY.
GOT TROUBLE HERE FOR SURE

LAURA. My name is Laura Vesper. Adrian Wasp's personal assistant. Wasp Enterprises needs your help. We're in a very vulnerable position.

SAM. Somebody lose a suspender button?

BUDDY. Somehow she managed to keep a straight face.

LAURA. Tell me, Mr. Galahad—are you always this charming with your clients?

SAM. (*Pouring himself a drink.*) You'll have to forgive me, Miss Vesper. My usual clientele isn't exactly the executive type. They're more the stagger-into-your-office-and-bleed-on-your-carpet type.

LAURA. I hope I haven't disappointed you.

SAM. No, you're doing fine. What does Wasp Enterprises want with me?

LAURA. I'm sure you've heard. Night before last, Mr. Wasp—took his own life.

SAM. On Mansion Hill—I've seen the papers.

LAURA. It was tragic.

SAM. Death usually is, even when you don't own half the city. Where do I come in?

LAURA. (*Taking out a photo.*) This is Jennifer Wasp. Mr. Wasp's daughter. And only heir.

BUDDY.
RAINDROPS ON THE WINDOW BEAT A SAD
    TATTOO
AND THE DAY WENT FROM GRAY TO A KINDA
    BLUE
SAM LOOKED KINDA FUNNY AS HE PUT OUT HIS
    CIGARETTE
YOU CAN RUN BUT YOU CAN'T HIDE AND YOU
    NEVER CAN FORGET

SAM. Forget about ships. This face could have launched a thousand rockets. She had hair the color of moonlight on topaz. And a mouth that would have sent Shakespeare thumbing through a thesaurus.

LAURA. It's an old photo. She's aged.

SAM. Haven't we all.

LAURA. Mr. Galahad, there is a board meeting next week. I must see Jennifer before that meeting.

SAM. What's stopping you?

LAURA./BUDDY. She's disappeared. Mr. Galahad.

SAM/LAURA/BUDDY.
DON'T KNOW WHAT I EXPECTED
GOT TROUBLE HERE FOR SURE

LAURA.
THE DETECTIVE

SAM.
THE DETECTED

ALL.
WHEN DID THE LINES BEGIN TO BLUR?

SAM. Names.

BUDDY. Dates.

SAM. Places.

BUDDY. Numbers.

SAM/BUDDY. Facts!

LAURA. Jennifer tried to call her father on the afternoon of his death.

SAM. What time was this?

LAURA. Around six. I told her that Mr. Wasp had just left for the airport and was there anything I could do, but she said no—and hung up.

SAM. She say where she was calling from?

LAURA. The penthouse at Wasp Tower.

SAM. That where she was living?

LAURA. For the past month. Before that, on Mansion Hill with her father. Mr. Wasp was against the move.

SAM. I'm not surprised. You had a little trouble at Wasp Tower.

LAURA. Trouble?

SAM. The protests over the demolition of the Metro Concert Hall.

LAURA. A minor annoyance.

SAM. Your security boys put six protesters in the hospital.

LAURA. We don't like being annoyed.

SAM. I'll keep that in mind. Why'd Jenny leave Mansion Hill?

LAURA. One of her whims. Suddenly she was interested in the corporation. Frankly, she was a nuisance. Looking through old files, asking questions.

SAM. And now she's disappeared.

LAURA. That's why I'm so worried. Mr. Galahad, you must understand—Jennifer is ... very fragile.

SAM. We all have our breaking points, Miss Vesper.

LAURA. But Jennifer needs protection. She had a breakdown, almost ten years ago. It left her—unstable. Scarred. Now ... after what's happened, I'm afraid ...

LAURA/BUDDY. She may do something desperate.

SAM. If I take the case, would I be working for you or Wasp Enterprises?

LAURA. Why don't we keep this personal?

SAM. Give me twenty bucks. (*SHE does.*) I'll keep this as a retainer and send you a bill for the rest. I'm working for you. Who you work for is your business.

LAURA. I'll be staying on Mansion Hill. You can get in touch with me there.

SAM. When I have something.

LAURA/BUDDY. You will find her—won't you, Mr. Galahad?

SAM. Yes. (*LAURA exits.*) And then she was gone. Trailing perfume like a whispered prayer. I listened as the high heels faded to a white noise. I was alone with Jenny. (*SAM is staring at the photo.*)

[Music Cue #4: FACTS!]

BUDDY. You know her?
SAM. I knew her.
BUDDY. You loved her?
SAM. Never mind.
BUDDY. She left you?
SAM. I lost her. She was the one I couldn't find.
Now I find anything for anyone
All you gotta do is call
I'm right here in my office
At the dark end of the hall
(Singing.)
SPIDER IN THE BASIN
BOURBON IN THE DRAWER
PAINT PEELING ON THE CEILING
AND STAINS ON THE FLOOR
I DUSTED WITH MY SHIRT 'N
HUNG A CURTAIN UP WITH TACKS
THIS IS THE PLACE
I'VE COME TO FACE THE FACTS

I STICK TO THE FACTS
NOTHING ELSE IS REAL
IT'S A MATTER OF FACTS
NO MATTER WHAT I FEEL
I'M WALKING DOWN THESE MEAN STREETS
I'M STEPPIN' ON THE CRACKS
I'VE TRADED IN MY FICTION
FOR THE FACTS

I HEAR THE RAUCOUS LAUGHTER OF THE
    STRONG MAN
BUT IF YOU THINK I LAUGH ALONG YOU'VE
    GOT THE WRONG MAN
I TAKE IT ON THE JAW WHEN LAW AND ORDER
    TURN THEIR BACKS

WHEN ALL I'M LEFT WITH ARE THE FACTS

I STICK TO THE FACTS.
IT'S THE LIFE I CHOOSE
I GOT NOTHING BUT FACTS
AND NOTHING LEFT TO LOSE
I'M GOING TO FIND HER THIS TIME
I'LL STOP HER IN HER TRACKS
I COULDN'T FIND YOU WITH LOVE
BUT I'LL FIND YOU WITH THE FACTS

(After the number, BUDDY begins to play as SAM looks out the window.)

[Music Cue #4A: WASP TOWER]

SAM. Wasp Tower. Jenny's last known address. It stood on the site of the old Metro Concert Hall. I could see it from my office window. Thirty stories worth of greed and gold-tinted glass that marred the face of the city like a cut-rate nose job. (*SAM puts on his hat and coat.*) Since I had a client, I took a taxi to Wasp Tower. I didn't take a gun. I didn't think I'd need one to talk to a doorman.
BUDDY. (*Puts on a doorman's cap and pulls a gun. HE points it at Sam. As DOORMAN.*) Hold it right there, chum. C'mon, you know the routine.

(SAM assumes the position. The DOORMAN frisks him.)

SAM. The name's Galahad. I'm a sleuth.
DOORMAN. (*Puts the gun away.*) Private license, huh? You workin'?
SAM. I'm looking for Jennifer Wasp.
DOORMAN. Miss Wasp isn't in.
SAM. I know that. That's why I'm looking for her.
DOORMAN. Wise guy, huh?

SAM. Maybe to some.

DOORMAN. Look pal, we got rules here, see? The tenants like their privacy. And they don't pay me to have any ideas.

SAM. What's an idea run in this neighborhood?

DOORMAN. Twenty bucks.

(SAM hands him a twenty, which HE places in the "tips" glass.)

DOORMAN. It was the day before yesterday. Around six. Miss Wasp comes in with an armful of paperwork.

SAM. Paperwork?

DOORMAN. Yeah. One of those big manila envelopes, crammed full. She goes up to her penthouse. Five minutes later she comes back down, gets me to call the limo, and off she goes.

SAM. You catch where she was going?

DOORMAN. She says, "Take me to the airport."

SAM. She say anything else?

DOORMAN. Yeah, that's why I remember it. While we're waitin' for the limo, I notice she's still got the paperwork. So I says to her—just to make conversation—how she's really puttin' in the overtime, you know, keepin' her eye on Wasp Enterprises. And she says to me, "It's about time somebody did." Next day I read in the papers how Wasp took the big shortcut.

SAM. You making something out of that?

DOORMAN. Not me, brother. They don't pay me to be smart.

SAM. I'm not sure they could. I'm going to take a look around the penthouse.

DOORMAN. Take a hike! I could get into a lot of trouble just talkin' to you.

SAM. *(Grabbing him by the lapels.)* The way I figure it, we're working for the same people. It wouldn't exactly break my heart to let 'em know how anxious you were to roll over and do tricks for a lousy double sawbuck.

DOORMAN. Hey, take it easy! You don't have to get tough. I mean, if somebody was to go up to Miss Wasp's penthouse while I was busy sorting the mail, for instance ... I wouldn't have to know anything about it, would I?

(BUDDY takes off the Doorman's cap and begins to play.)

[Music Cue #5: IN THE PENTHOUSE]

BUDDY.
HE TOOK A PRIVATE ELEVATOR TO THE PENTHOUSE FLOOR
THERE'S A PRIVATE LITTLE FOYER. NO NUMBER ON THE DOOR
IT'S ALL VERY PRIVATE AND SO HE SET ABOUT IT
HE BROKE IN WITH A CREDIT CARD
SAM.
DON'T LEAVE HOME WITHOUT IT
DON'T KNOW WHAT I EXPECTED
BUT ALL I SAW WAS ...
FURNITURE OVERTURNED!
PAPERS SCATTERED AND RIPPED!
BUDDY.
JENNY.
SAM.
TORN!
BUDDY.
JENNY!
SAM.
GONE!
BUDDY.
JENNY!!

SAM.
SHATTERED!
BUDDY/SAM.
DON'T KNOW WHAT I EXPECTED
GOT TROUBLE HERE FOR SURE

SAM. Then a floorboard creaked and the back of my head exploded. They say you see stars, but they say a lot of things. What I felt was a Mariachi band tuning up in my stomach. I heard footsteps a hundred miles away, and a door slammed somewhere in Tibet. Then the world went black, and I went with it. I dreamed I was in a falling elevator with a wasp dressed like a doorman. And a stranger with hair like moonlight on topaz.

(SAM finally falls unconscious as BUDDY finishes playing.)

SAM. I woke up in the gutter. That was all right. I'd been there before. Only this time I had company.

(The BLONDE has entered dressed as a bag lady. This is the PRINCESS.)

PRINCESS. I didn't think you'd last long.
SAM. What?
PRINCESS. I seen you go in. I says to myself, "Princess, that guy don't belong in there."
SAM. *(Rubbing his head.)* I can think of at least one guy who'd agree with you.
PRINCESS. You don't belong in there, Sam!
SAM. How'd you know my name?
PRINCESS. Sam, Dick, Harry ... it's all the same to me.
SAM. Listen, you didn't happen to see anybody suspicious coming out of Wasp Tower just now?
PRINCESS. You mean besides you? No, I didn't see nobody. I got a lot on my mind. I got things I'm supposed to remember.

SAM. Oh yeah?

PRINCESS. You think it's so easy, you try it. (*Remembering and pointing out the memories.*) The old brownstone. The front stoop. The railing. The rust spot. You can't leave nothing out! The tree ... the sidewalk... the blonde with the suitcase ...

BUDDY. (*Prompting her.*) The concert hall.

PRINCESS. The concert hall ...

SAM. Wait! What blonde with the suitcase?

PRINCESS. Night before last! You gotta remember these things, Sam!

SAM. You were here night before last?

PRINCESS. No, I was sippin' cocktails on Mansion Hill. Yeah, I was here. I seen her. Blonde, like me.

SAM. What time?

PRINCESS. It was late. 'Round midnight. She gets out of the cab. She's weavin'. She'd had a few. She goes inside. When she comes out, she's carrying the suitcase. I seen her. She didn't see me.

SAM. (*Showing her the photo.*) Is this the woman you saw?

PRINCESS. No. You sure you're lookin' for the right blonde?

SAM. Her name's Jennifer Wasp. She lives in the penthouse ...

PRINCESS. I never seen her. It's cold. I'm so cold.

SAM. (*Giving her a card.*) Look, if you remember anything else, get in touch. Or if you need anything ...

(*SAM starts to check his pockets, then realizes he gave the doorman the last of his money. BUDDY takes a bill from his "tips" glass and gives it to Sam. SAM hands it to the Princess and turns to go.*)

PRINCESS. I never seen her.

(*SAM looks at her a moment. BUDDY begins to play. SAM exits.*)

[Music Cue #6: LOOSE CHANGE]

PRINCESS.
SHE'S BETTER OFF LOST
LIKE I AM
BETTER OFF LOST
SHE'S HISTORY
NEVER SEEN HER
NEVER SEEN HER FACE
INVISIBLE
LIKE ME ...

SPARE SOME CHANGE, BROTHER?
GOT A CIGARETTE, SISTER?
DON'T TURN AWAY, MISTER,
OR I'LL DISAPPEAR.
SPARE SOME CHANGE? LOOSE CHANGE?

SPARE SOME CHANGE, BUDDY?
GOT A DIME, LADY?
SPARE SOME TIME AND
I WON'T DISAPPEAR
FOR A CHANGE.
SPARE SOME CHANGE?

BETTER OFF LOST
INVISIBLE
DIDN'T SEE ME
DIDN'T EVEN TRY
INVISIBLE
NOW I ...

THINK IT'S STRANGE HOW
YOU COME AND GO. NOW
YOU SEE ME, NOW YOU DON'T
SEE ME DISAPPEAR.
THERE'S NO CHANGE.

I SEE YOU PASSING BY
I SEE WHAT YOU DENY
SEE YOUR GUILT, YOUR LIES, AND YOUR FEAR
SO RUN, JENNY, YOU DISAPPEAR.
KINDA STRANGE ...
SPARE SOME CHANGE?
LOOSE CHANGE?

(BLACKOUT on the PRINCESS. BUDDY plays as the LIGHTS come up on SAM. [Music Cue #6A: AFTER LOOSE CHANGE])

SAM. I walked back to my office. I was cold, my head hurt, and I didn't know a goddamn thing. I felt I was making real progress.

BUDDY. (*Stops playing.*) Who searched the penthouse?

SAM. Who was the blonde with the suitcase?

BUDDY. What about the paperwork?

SAM. What I wanted were some answers. And about three fingers of Old Crow.

BUDDY. (*Puts on a fedora. As COP.*) What's new, Galahad?

SAM. What I got was a visit from Metro's finest. Hello, Lieutenant. What an unpleasant surprise.

COP. You look like hell.

SAM. (*Pouring himself a drink.*) Stick around, I'm about to look a lot worse. I'd ask you to join me but I know you're on duty.

COP. (*Taking Sam's drink.*) Siddown, shamus. (*HE throws back the drink.*) Let's you and me have a little chat.

SAM. Is it all right if I have a cigarette—or will you shoot it out of my mouth?

COP. Don't get cute, Galahad. I hate it when you get cute. What were you doing at Wasp Tower?

SAM. Working on a case.

COP. You got no case. You're out of it, you hear me?

SAM. I'm listening.

COP. Well, listen to this—it's a murder case. And Jennifer Wasp is the prime suspect.

SAM. Murder?

COP. You're not so cute anymore.

SAM. The papers said suicide.

COP. It was murder. Wasp was holding the gun. alright. But I smell a set-up.

SAM. No suicide note?

COP. And not a bank note out of place.

SAM. All neat and tidy.

COP. Tidied up with perfume. Then we come to find Wasp booked a seat for the red-eye. The flight left two hours after he was dead. I don't like it.

SAM. There's not much to like.

COP. Then you show up. I like it a whole lot less. Who's your client?

SAM. Thanks for dropping by, Lieutenant.

COP. Jennifer Wasp?

SAM. You owe me for the bourbon.

COP. I'm wise to you, Galahad. I know who you are.

SAM. Yeah?

COP. You're a two-bit keyhole peeper. You left town ten years ago. Nobody seems to know why. I figure there was trouble.

SAM. There usually is.

COP. So why come back?

SAM. I wanted to be alone.

COP. Alone? There's over two million people in the city.

SAM. I misread the census.

COP. *(Grabbing Sam.)* I'm warning you, Galahad. Murder on Mansion Hill is a little out of your weight class. And I'd just as soon pull your licence as look at you. Sooner.

SAM. Please, Lieutenant. You're scarin' me to death.

COP. You wanna see how scary I can be? Keep it up. I'll make your worst nightmare look like a wet dream.

SAM. I had a wisecrack all ready, but I hated to spoil a good exit line.

(BUDDY takes off the fedora.)

SAM. I took out the photo of Jenny.

[Music Cue #6B: PHOTO OF JENNY]

BUDDY. (*As Sam looks at photo.*) It didn't look like the face of someone who'd put a gun to her father's head and pull the trigger.

SAM. But then again ...

BUDDY. Yes?

SAM. I didn't know what somebody who'd do that would look like.

BUDDY. Good point.

SAM. Ten years is a long time.

BUDDY. People change.

SAM. I just had this feeling.

BUDDY. Call it a hunch.

SAM. All right, a hunch.

BUDDY. Thanks.

SAM. But I don't like hunches. Hunches are for suckers. I needed to talk to Laura Vesper. [Music Cue #7: MANSION HILL] It's a short drive from the office to Mansion Hill. Not far at all. Only about a half a mile. And a couple of million dollars.

SAM.
I'M TALKING 'BOUT A PLACE
ON THE RIGHT SIDE OF THE TRACKS
BEYOND THE COUNTRY CLUB
BEYOND THE INCOME TAX
WHO CAN BE UNHAPPY THERE?
WHO CAN SING THE BLUES?
MUFFY LOST AN EARRING

MAKES THE FRONT PAGE NEWS
I GOT AN INVITATION
    BUDDY.
DON'T TELL ME, LET ME GUESS
YOU WERE CORDIALLY INVITED
TO TIDY UP A MESS
    SAM.
THEY NEVER PAY THE PIPER
BUT THEY ALWAYS PAY MY BILL
    SAM/BUDDY.
WHO ELSE WOULD DO THE DIRTY WORK
ON MANSION HILL

MANSION HILL, MANSION HILL
    BOTH.
MONEY TO BURN
    SAM.
TIME TO KILL
    BOTH.
MANSION HILL, MANSION HILL
    SAM.
NEVER LIVED THERE
    BUDDY.
NEVER WILL

THE GRASS IS ALWAYS GREENER
    SAM.
THE GRAPE'S ARE NEVER SOUR
    BUDDY.
THE KING IS IN HIS CASTLE
    SAM.
THE DAMSEL'S IN HER TOWER
    BUDDY.
IF YOU TRY TO SAVE HER
YOU'RE GONNA CATCH A CHILL
    BOTH.
THE ALTITUDE'LL GET TO YOU
ON MANSION HILL

MANSION HILL, MANSION HILL,
MONEY TO BURN
  BUDDY.
TIME TO KILL
  BOTH.
MANSION HILL, MANSION HILL
  SAM.
NEVER LIVED THERE
  BOTH.
NEVER WILL

(SAM has arrived on Mansion Hill. LAURA enters wearing a silky dressing gown.)

LAURA. Mr. Galahad, thank God you're here! The police ...

SAM. I know. They paid me a visit too.

LAURA. You? What did you tell them?

SAM. Not much. But then again, I don't know much of anything.

LAURA. I told you ...

SAM. I remember what you told me. You knew Wasp was murdered.

LAURA. No.

SAM. Did Jenny kill her father?

LAURA. No! I don't know.

SAM. Look, I want to help you, but I can't unless you level with me.

LAURA. I was the one who found Mr. Wasp.

SAM. You?!

LAURA. I'd been working late in the office that night. Mr. Wasp phoned. He asked me to come here. He wanted my opinion on some paperwork. I got here a little before ten ... and I found him. And then I found this.

*(LAURA takes out a compact and shows it to Sam.
BUDDY provides underscoring. [Music Cue #7A:
JENNY-LAURA INCIDENTAL])*

BUDDY. A woman's compact; white gold, with a single diamond inset. Its mirror splintered. Shattered. Seven years bad luck.
SAM. Jenny's?
LAURA. A Christmas present from her father. I picked it out myself.
SAM. She was here that night. I don't suppose you mentioned that to the cops.
LAURA. I was just trying to ... I wanted ... to protect the family.
SAM. You re a damn fool.

(THEY kiss as BUDDY swells the music.)

LAURA.
DON'T KNOW WHAT I EXPECTED
SAM.
GOT TROUBLE HERE FOR SURE
BUDDY.
JENNY ...
SAM. Tell me about the paperwork.
LAURA. ... paperwork...?
SAM. The paperwork Wasp wanted your opinion on. The reason you came here that night.
LAURA. You're all business, aren't you Sam?
SAM. Tell me about it, Laura.
LAURA. There was no paperwork.
SAM. But there was a woman at Wasp Tower that night, a blonde.
LAURA. Jennifer?
SAM. I don't think so. She arrived around midnight. She'd been hitting the sauce pretty hard.
LAURA. Carol Indigo!
SAM. Go on.

LAURA. She and Mr. Wasp had been ... She calls herself a "singer." What was she doing at the penthouse?

SAM. I was kind of hoping you'd tell me. I'll be in touch. (*SAM turns to go.*)

LAURA. You still don't trust me, do you?

SAM. I'm trying to.

(*SAM leaves the house. BUDDY begins to play.*)

[Music Cue #8: SHADOWPLAY]

SAM. Sure I trusted her, but I was a sap. I trusted everybody—doormen, cops with bourbon breath, bag ladies ... I was through playing the sap. It was dark out now. And the gray mist of the morning had given way to a ceiling of cold, unblinking stars. I went around to the back of the house.

(*SAM peeps through the window at Laura as BUDDY sings.*)

BUDDY.
HE WAS A SOLITARY MAN WHOSE FOOTSTEPS
LEFT NO TRACES IN THE SNOW
HER WINDOW WAS A SCREEN IN THE DARKNESS
HER SECRET LIFE A SILENT PICTURE SHOW
SAM.
SHADOW, BLUE SHADOW
YOU GOT A NEW SHADOW
ONE STEP BEHIND YOU
WHEN YOU WALK DOWN THE STREET
DODGING YOUR GLANCES
RETREATS AND ADVANCES
YES, THIS DANCE IS YOURS
AND I WON'T MISS A BEAT

BUDDY.
HE THOUGHT THAT HE WAS FAR BEYOND
   TEMPTATION
INSENSIBLE TO LOVE'S EMBRACE
HE WATCHES WITH RELUCTANT FASCINATION
HER SILHOUETTE AGAINST THE CURTAIN LACE
   SAM.
SHADOW, BLUE SHADOW
YOU GOT A NEW SHADOW
YOU CAN'T ESCAPE ME
I WON'T LET YOU GO
I'M IN YOUR SHOES NOW
SO GO WHERE YOU CHOOSE NOW
WHATEVER THE RUSE NOW
YOUR SHADOW WILL KNOW

*(The LIGHTS fade on SAM, still peering through the
   window. BUDDY continues to play.)*

[Music Cue #9: SKELETONS]

LAURA.
IN THE HOUSE HIGH ON THE HILL
CERTAIN DOORS WERE ALWAYS LOCKED
AND NO ONE CAME TO ANSWER THEM
NO MATTER HOW YOU KNOCKED
AND CERTAIN QUESTIONS ALWAYS STIRRED
A PUZZLED LOOK, AN ANGRY WORD
IN THE HOUSE HIGH ON THE HILL
I OVERHEARD

RATTLING OF SKELETONS
IN THE DEAD OF NIGHT
THROUGH THE DISTANT HALLWAYS
ALWAYS OUT OF SIGHT
RATTLING OF SKELETONS
I HEARD THEM WHISPERING MY NAME
NO ONE ELSE COULD HEAR THEM

BUT I FEARED THEM JUST THE SAME

FOR THE MAN HIGH ON THE HILL
DEVOTION WAS MY TASK
DEVOTION, LOVE, AND LOYALTY
WHAT MORE COULD ONE MAN ASK?
AND I WAS BLIND, I DIDN'T TRY
TO SEE THE TRUTH, OR SEE THE LIE
THEN IN THE HOUSE HIGH ON THE HILL
I WATCHED HIM DIE

NOW I'LL DANCE WITH SKELETONS
I'LL TAKE THEM IN MY ARMS AND SAY
I AM NOT AFRAID OF SKELETONS
I CAN KEEP YOU LOCKED AWAY
NOW I'LL DANCE WITH SKELETONS
A SKELETON IS JUST A FRAME
FOR THE SOUL TO HANG ITS HEART IN
OH, I LOVED HIM JUST THE SAME

(BLACKOUT. LIGHTS up on SAM.)

[Music Cue #9A: AFTER SKELETONS I]

SAM. When Laura Vesper killed the light, I was where I usually am—alone in the dark. Just a little man peeping into a big house. And seeing only his own, tired eyes in the window's dark mirror. Then it happened.

BUDDY. (*As ROCCO.)* Peek-a-boo, gumshoe.

SAM. I felt the hot breath in my ear and the cold steel on the back of my neck. I felt like a chump.

ROCCO. The boss wants to see you.

SAM. How's it going, Rocco? Still having trouble with that pesky prehensile thumb?

ROCCO. Start movin'!

SAM. A dark sedan was waiting for us at the bottom of the drive. Rocco wedged himself behind the wheel while I climbed in back. I was nose to cologne with Joe Paisley.

(BUDDY puts on a homburg.)

BUDDY. *(As PAISLEY.)* Rocco, take us to the airport. It's been a long time, Sammy.
SAM. Not long enough. What's on your mind, Joe.
PAISLEY. Business.
SAM. I don't do business with crooks. *(To audience.)* Paisley slapped me across the mouth. *(PAISLEY does so.)* He probably thought it was hard.
PAISLEY. You got guts, Sammy. That's why I want you to work for me. I got a little problem. Outta town. Pays a thousand a day.
SAM. Not interested.
PAISLEY. Get interested.
SAM. This wouldn't have anything to do with Adrian Wasp, would it?
PAISLEY. Come on, Sammy, be smart for once. You got guts, but you got no brains.

(PAISLEY pours drinks for Sam and himself.)

SAM. Did you push the button on Wasp?
PAISLEY. Now you're being dumb again. Wasp and me did business.
SAM. Wasp was dirty? *(SAM drinks.)*
PAISLEY. We did business. Strictly legitimate. It's a shame what had to happen to the old concert hall. But what can I tell you? Ancient history.
SAM. How does Jennifer Wasp figure in?
PAISLEY. Let's just say it's in my interest that the daughter stays lost. *(PAISLEY begins to speak in slow motion.)* How's your drink, Sammy? You don't look so good.
SAM. You doped me.

PAISLEY. (*Returning to normal speech.*) Just a little insurance policy. Rocco, pull over.

SAM. I pitched forward, grasping for the bottle. Rocco turned around and I brought my hand down hard. In the movies, it's always the bottle that breaks.

PAISLEY. You're a dead man, Galahad!

SAM. But I was out of the car and running. [Music Cue #9B: AFTER SKELETONS II] I was sweating like a busted fire hydrant, and my pulse was a drum solo. The world became a vortex of swirling shadows ... and a red neon eye, blinking ... swirling ... red ... blinking ... shadow ... sinking ... (*SAM had stumbled into the Red Eye Lounge. HE falls unconscious at a table.*)

BUDDY. (*Plays a bass octave tremelo.*) Ladies and gentlemen, the Red Eye Lounge is proud to present ... the one ... the only ... the lovely ... Miss Carol Indigo!

(The blonde enters wearing a drop-dead red dress. This is CAROL INDIGO. SHE's had a few.)

CAROL. Hit it.

[Music Cue #10: THE BLONDE SONG]

THERE ARE BLONDES
AND THERE ARE BLONDES
AND IT'S ALMOST LIKE A JOKE
YOU BREATH THEM IN LIKE PERFUME
YOU BLOW THEM OUT LIKE SMOKE
YOU POUR THEM IN YOUR COFFEE
YOU BOUNCE THEM ON YOUR KNEE
WELL, THERE ARE BLONDES,
AND THERE ARE BLONDES,
BUT YOU'LL NEVER FIND A BLONDE LIKE ME

YOU KNOW I'VE BEEN A
COOL BLONDE, CRUEL BLONDE
PLAY-YOU-FOR-A-FOOL BLONDE

DUMB BLONDE, DUM-DE-DUM BLONDE
"HOW KIND OF YOU TO COME" BLONDE
STATIC BLONDE, ACROBATIC BLONDE
IDIOSYNCRATIC BLONDE
BUT YOU'LL NEVER FIND A BLONDE LIKE ME

YOU WON'T FIND ME DOCKSIDE
HAIR FULL OF PEROXIDE
LIPSTICK IN A SMEAR
OR FLYING WITH THE JET SET
THE USED-TO-BE BRUNETTE SET
YOU WON'T FIND ME, DEAR
IT'S VERY CLEAR

I'VE BEEN A
SAINT BLONDE, QUAINT BLONDE
CATCH-ME-OR-I'LL-FAINT BLONDE
DOUR BLONDE, COLD SHOWER BLONDE
"HAVE YOU READ SHOPENHAUER?" BLONDE
BLEACH BLONDE, ON THE BEACH BLONDE
"ONCE MORE INTO THE BREACH" BLONDE
OH, YOU'LL NEVER FIND A BLONDE LIKE ME

I'M NOT A BLONDE WHO'LL CHEEP AND
    TWITTER
NOT UNTIL YOU WANT TO HIT HER
OR TAKE IT ON THE LAM
I'M NOT YOUR LITTLE SISTER
WON'T YOU LISTEN TO ME, MISTER?
LISTEN TO ME, SAM.

I'M JUST A LOST BLONDE, TEMPEST-TOSSED
    BLONDE
GOT-MY-WIRES-CROSSED BLONDE
WANTED BLONDE, HAUNTED BLONDE
TRY-TO-STAY-UNDAUNTED BLONDE
BRUISED BLONDE, ILL-USED BLONDE
UTTERLY CONFUSED BLONDE

OH, WON'T YOU FIND THE BLONDE THAT'S ME?

(After the number, CAROL sits with a drink at a corner table. A PLANE is heard overhead. BUDDY tickles the ivories.)

[Music Cue #10A: COCKTAIL MUSIC I]

SAM. (*Waking up.*) Gimme a drink.
BUDDY. You missed last call.
SAM. Black coffee.
BUDDY. Right.
SAM. Piping hot.
BUDDY. You got it.
SAM. When it gets here, pour it over my head, willya?
BUDDY. Sure thing
SAM. (*Listening to music.*) That's nice. What is it?
BUDDY. Just something I'm fooling around with.

(SAM goes over to the piano. HE pours himself a drink. BUDDY watches.)

BUDDY. Working on a case, Sam?
SAM. (*Tossing back the drink.*) Right now all I'm working on is this bottle.
BUDDY. Looks like the bottle's working on you.
SAM. It's a "missing person."
BUDDY. A girl.
SAM. Maybe she killed her father.
BUDDY. But you don't think so.
SAM. The cops want me out.
BUDDY. Yeah?
SAM. The bad guys want me out.
BUDDY. But you don't want out.
SAM. No. I'm too far in. (*SAM listens as BUDDY plays.*) Where do they do, Buddy? The dreams you're always chasing? I look, and I look, and I look ...

BUDDY. Maybe you just like to look.

SAM. What about you?

BUDDY. Me?

SAM. What are you looking for?

BUDDY. I had a crazy dream, once. [Music Cue #10B: THE VIRTUOSO THEME] Me on a big stage ... in a big hall ... Buddy Toupee ... THE VIRTUOSO ... Crazy, huh?

[Music Cue #11: CHILDHOOD DAYS]

SAM. Dreams aren't crazy, Buddy. These days ... they're all we've got.

BUDDY.
BRING ME BACK MY CHILDHOOD DAYS
THE SKY WHEN IT WAS BLUE
RAIN WHEN IT WAS PURE
AND LOVE WHEN IT WAS TRUE
I'VE GOT A POCKET FULL OF TICKETS
FOR A LOTTERY I DIDN'T WIN
AN ALBUM FULL OF PHOTOGRAPHS
OF PLACES THAT I'VE NEVER BEEN.

SAM.
BRING BACK THE GIRL WHO MIGHT HAVE
    STAYED
WHOSE ARMS WERE NEVER COLD
WHO NEVER SEEMED AFRAID
OF FEELING PAIN OR GROWING OLD
I'VE GOT A POCKET FULL OF LETTERS
I NEVER SENT TO ANYONE
A PLACE THAT ACHES WHENEVER I
SMELL HYACINTH OR CINNAMON
SHE DISAPPEARED WITHOUT A TRACE
SHE NEVER TOLD ME WHAT I'D DONE
AND EVERYWHERE I SEE HER FACE
RETURNING FROM OBLIVION
BUT THAT WAS SO LONG AGO
IT'S HARD TO KNOW

WAS IT OVER?
HAD IT JUST BEGUN?

BUDDY.	**SAM.**
A POCKET FULL OF MELODY	A POCKET FULL OF HAPPY ENDS
ANY TUNE IN ANY KEY	I LOST THEM ALL EXCEPT
THE SOUVENIRS	THE SOUVENIRS I KEPT
	THE SONGS SHE SANG
THAT SOMEONE BROUGHT	
BUT NOT FOR ME	THE TEARS SHE WEPT

CAROL.
LOST BLONDE, TEMPEST-TOSSED BLONDE
GOT-MY-WIRES-CROSSES BLONDE
WANTED BLONDE, HAUNTED BLONDE
TRY-TO-STAY-UNDAUNTED BLONDE
I'VE GOT A POCKET FULL OF EVIDENCE
AGAINST THE CHILD I USED TO BE
THE PUNISHMENT MUST SUIT THE CRIME
THE CRIME WAS MY NAIVETY

(CAROL/SAM/BUDDY–Counterpoint.)

BUDDY.
A POCKET FULL OF MELODY
ANY TUNE IN ANY KEY
THE SOUVENIRS THAT SOMEONE BROUGHT
BUT NOT FOR ME
CAROL.
A POCKET FULL OF MISSING CLUES
YOU DISAPPEAR, YOU NEVER CHOOSE
THE SOUVENIRS I NEVER KEPT
I'LL NEVER LOSE
SAM.
A POCKET FULL OF HAPPY ENDS
I LOST THEM ALL EXCEPT
THE SOUVENIRS I KEPT

THE SONGS SHE SANG, THE TEARS SHE WEPT
  ALL.
GIVE ME BACK MY CHILDHOOD DAYS
  CAROL.
THE SKY WHEN IT WAS BLUE
  BUDDY.
AND FAITH WHEN IT WAS PURE
  SAM.
AND LOVE WHEN IT WAS TRUE
  ALL.
I'VE GOT A POCKET FULL OF MUSIC
I CAN'T REMEMBER HOW TO PLAY
I THOUGHT I KNEW IT ALL BY HEART
WHEN DID I LET IT FADE AWAY?
  CAROL.
IN THE NAME OF LOSS
  SAM.
IN THE NAME OF PAIN
  BUDDY.
IN THE NAME OF SHATTERED HOPES
  ALL.
GIVE ME BACK MY LIFE AGAIN!

(BUDDY continues to play as CAROL gets up to leave. SAM puts his head down on the table like Bogie in "Casablanca.")

SAM. Jenny.

(CAROL stops in the doorway and looks back at Sam. BUDDY catches her eye. SHE hesitates for a moment.)

CAROL. She's better off lost.

(THEY remain suspended for a moment. Then BUDDY turns to the audience.)

[Music Cue #12: TAKE A BREAK]

BUDDY.
TAKE A BREAK
HAVE A DRINK
I'LL BE BACK
IN A WINK
HAVE A DRINK
TAKE A BREAK
I GOTTA SHORT
CALL TO MAKE

NOW'S YOUR CHANCE
DON'T LET IT PASS
TO SLIP A TIP
INTO THE BRANDY GLASS

(The LIGHTS fade, leaving only a PIN SPOT on BUDDY.)

STRETCH YOUR LEGS
DON'T BE SHY
AS YOU KNOW
TIME WILL FLY
AND I'LL BE BACK
BEFORE YOU CAN SAY
"WHERE'S THAT KING OF THE KEYBOARD ...
BUDDY TOUPEE???!!!!"

BLACKOUT

End of ACT I

ACT II

DARKNESS. Maybe another PLANE takes off. A
PIANO ROLL. The LIGHTS come up on BUDDY.
[Music Cue #13: BUDDY TOUPEE—LIVE]

BUDDY.
For a limited time only!
Not available in stores!!
It's yours for only $19.95!!!
Don't miss this opportunity
To thrill to your favorite tunes!!!!
He croons!!!!!
It's Buddy Toupee—Live!!!!!!

Bring back your childhood days with ...
BRING ME BACK MY CHILDHOOD DAYS

And his moving rendition of ...
THERE ARE BLONDES
AND THERE ARE BLONDES
AND IT'S ALMOST LIKE A JOKE

But this offer's no joke. And what's more ... it's not
available in stores! And isn't that just what you'd expect
from Buddy Toupee?

DON'T KNOW WHAT I EXPECTED,
GOT TROUBLE HERE FOR SURE

But it's no trouble. Just call that toll-free number. Act
now to receive this autographed 8 x 10 glossy of Buddy.
It's a deal. and that's a fact!

I STICK TO THE FACTS,

43

NOTHING ELSE IS REAL

But this offer's real. And, once more ... it's not available in stores!! You think you've heard it all?? No!! There's more!! If you call today, we'll send you Buddy's Hits of Act Two!!! Including the mysterious ...

JENNY, OH YES I'VE SEEN JENNY

And the heart-warming ...
ORDER ANYTHING YOU WANT
ANYTHING YOUR HEART DESIRES

So order now! That toll-free number again: 1-800-922-2222. It's too good to be true! Requests are pouring in!! Just listen to those phones!!! (*BUDDY stops playing. There is absolute silence.*)
Yes! Buddy Toupee is ...
THE VIRTUOSO, OH SO FULL OF BEAUTY AND TRUTH

Visa and MasterCard accepted.

(*BLACKOUT. LIGHTS up on SAM. HE is at the same table where we left him at the end of Act I. HE slowly wakes up as BUDDY plays. HE is very hungover.*)

[Music Cue #14: GUNMETAL BLUES]

SAM.
WOKE UP THIS MORNING WITH A FREIGHT
  TRAIN IN MY HEAD
WOKE UP THIS MORNING WITH A FREIGHT
  TRAIN IN MY HEAD
WENT TO BED WITH A CASE OF WHISKEY
WOKE UP WITH THE BLUES INSTEAD

RAIN AND SMOKE, ICE AND ASHES

SHADOW OVER LONG EYELASHES
MEMORIES STAIN LIKE AN OLD TATTOO
AND INK IN THE RAIN RUNS A GUNMETAL BLUE

GUNMETAL BLUE'S THE COLOR OF A BRUISE
COLOR OF A PAIR OF EYES, A PAIR OF HIGH-
  HEELED SHOES
COLOR OF THE MORNING THROUGH A
  HANGOVER RAIN
I GOT THE GUNMETAL BLUES AGAIN

   It was dawn when I left the Red Eye. And the rain on
my face was a washrag full of straight pins. You can have
a hangover from other things than too-many-drinks. I had
one from too-many-memories. Memories made me sick.

(SAM accompanies himself on a harmonica.)

WHEN A WOMAN SAYS SHE LOVES YOU, SHE'S
  STRINGING YOU ALONG
WHEN A WOMAN SAYS SHE LOVES YOU, SHE'S
  STRINGING YOU ALONG
IT'S THE SAME OLD STORY
IT'S THE SAME OLD SONG

GUNMETAL BLUE'S THE COLOR OF A BRUISE
COLOR OF A PAIR OF EYES, A PAIR OF HIGH-
  HEELED SHOES
COLOR OF A MORNING THROUGH A HANGOVER
  RAIN
I GOT THE GUNMETAL BLUES AGAIN.

GUNMETAL BLUE'S THE COLOR OF A BRUISE
COLOR OF A PAIR OF EYES, A PAIR OF HIGH-
  HEELED SHOES
COLOR OF THE MORNING THROUGH A
  HANGOVER RAIN
I GOT THE GUNMETAL BLUES AGAIN

BAD NEWS
I GOT THE GUNMETAL BLUES

SAM. I tried hailing a cab out on the airport strip. It didn't take much longer than a trip to the post office.

BUDDY. (*Picks up a serving tray and holds it like a steering wheel.*) Where to?

SAM. Downtown. (*SAM climbs into the "taxi." HE sits behind Buddy.*) And keep an eye on the rearview mirror. I don't care much for parades.

BUDDY. Okay by me.

SAM. Paisley was right. I hadn't been smart.

BUDDY. (*Putting on Paisley's hat.*) "You got guts, but you got no brains."

SAM. If Wasp was dirty ...

BUDDY. "We did business."

SAM. And Jenny found out about it

BUDDY. "Let's just say it's in my interest that the daughter stays lost."

SAM. Then Paisley was looking for her too.

BUDDY. "Just a little insurance policy."

SAM. But what if the cops were right?

BUDDY. (*Putting on the Cop's hat.*) "It's a murder case. And Jennifer Wasp is the prime suspect."

SAM. Could I really turn Jenny over to the cops?

BUDDY. "Don't get cute, Galahad."

SAM. That is, if I ever found her.

BUDDY. "I hate it when you get cute."

SAM. I had the cab drop me in the alley behind my office. Just in case Joe Paisley decided to throw me a welcome home party.

(*The PRINCESS appears.*)

PRINCESS. Psst, Sam! I been waiting for you.
SAM. Princess? What are you doing here?

PRINCESS. I remembered somethin'. The blonde with the suitcase—you ever find her?

SAM. No, I haven't found her. I haven't found anybody.

PRINCESS. I thought you were supposed to be a detective.

SAM. Don't let the trench coat fool you, I'm just expecting rain.

PRINCESS. You got trouble, Sam. Good thing you got me. I remembered. When she gets out of the taxi, I hit her up for some change. She gave me this ...

(PRINCESS pulls a cassette tape from one of her shopping bags and hands it to SAM.)

SAM. *(Reading.)* "Buddy Toupee—Live!!!"

BUDDY. Obviously a connoisseur.

PRINCESS. *(Pointing to the label.)* It's not available in stores.

SAM. There might be a reason for that. *(SAM offers the Princess her tape back.)*

PRINCESS. Keep it, Sam, I think it's a clue. Besides ... *(SHE speaks confidentially.)* ... it's not really my style.

BUDDY. Everybody's a critic

PRINCESS. I got my own music. *(SHE touches her heart.)* [Music Cue #14A: AFTER GUNMETAL BLUES] In here. I don't forget. The old concert hall. Remember, Sam. Remember the music! It's gone. *(BUDDY has stopped playing.)* Wasp took it away. History. The concert hall ... the Princess ... even Wasp, now. You're lookin' for his daughter, aren't you.

SAM. I thought you didn't know who she was.

PRINCESS. I said I never seen her. I know who she is. There's lots of ways to disappear. I know. It's like you're somebody else. And who you used to be is gone. If it was me you were lookin' for, you'd walk right by me.

SAM. Doesn't mean I'd stop looking.

PRINCESS. Maybe you're right. Maybe nobody wanted to find me that much. Tell Jenny the Princess says goodbye.

(BUDDY begins to play. [Music Cue #14B: BEFORE I'M THE ONE THAT GOT AWAY])

SAM. I watched her down the alley. Shopping bags and forgotten clothes. It's funny the things you notice, when you take the time to look—the Princess staring at her face in a mirror. Like she was asking directions.

(LIGHTS fade on SAM.)

[Music Cue #15: I'M THE ONE THAT GOT AWAY]

PRINCESS.
DID YOU KNOW THE STRANGER AT YOUR DOOR?
I CAN'T LET YOU SEE HER ANYMORE
SHE KNOWS WHO I AM
SHE KNOWS ALL I'VE DONE
AND IN TIME SHE'D TELL YOU

I'M THE ONE THAT GOT AWAY
GOT AWAY WITH LEADING ALL YOUR DREAMS
  ASTRAY
I'M THE ONE WHO FELL APART
AND BROKE YOUR HEART THAT DAY
THE ONE THAT GOT AWAY

I'M THE ONE WHO COULDN'T SEE
COULDN'T SEE A WAY
TO KEEP YOU CLOSE TO ME
I'M THE ONE WHO COULDN'T CHOOSE
TO LOVE AND LOSE
NOW I'M LOST AS I CAN BE

NOW I WANT YOU HERE BESIDE ME
YOU COULD HOLD ME, YOU COULD HIDE ME
I WANT TO LEAVE THE PAST BEHIND ME
IF ONLY I COULD LET YOU FIND ME

BUT I'M THE ONE THAT GOT AWAY
GOT AWAY WITH
MORE THAN I CAN SAY
AND I WONDER IF YOU KNOW
I LOVE YOU SO
THAT'S THE ROLE I'VE GOT TO PLAY
ALWAYS ON THE RUN.
YOU KNOW I'VE GOT TO STAY
THE ONE
THAT GOT AWAY

(LIGHTS fade on PRINCESS and come up on SAM.)

SAM. The office was pretty much how I'd left it. There were no blondes in the waiting room ...
BUDDY. No cops in the water closet ...
SAM. Nobody'd been there at all except the postman...
BUDDY. But he'd delivered a bombshell.

(BUDDY tosses SAM a big manila envelope—crammed full.)

SAM. The missing paperwork!

[Music Cue #15A:AFTER "I'M THE ONE THAT
GOT AWAY"]

(BUDDY begins to play as SAM goes through the contents of the envelope.)

SAM. It was all there. Wasp had been laundering Joe Paisley's dirty money. And Wasp Tower was the laundromat. There was enough evidence to put Wasp away for a long time. (*The MUSIC stops.*) And that's just what somebody had done. I put in a call to Laura Vesper.

(*SAM picks up a phone. BUDDY puts on an operator's earphone.*)

BUDDY. Wasp Enterprises, please hold. (*BUDDY plays some "hold" music.*) Only nineteen-ninety-five for your cassette of "Buddy Toupee—Live!!!" Send in your money now! Buddy Toup ... (*BUDDY stops abruptly.*) Wasp Enterprises, may I help you?
SAM. Laura Vesper.
BUDDY. Hold, please. (*More "hold" music.*) You've got to let Buddy Toupee into your life! Buddy Toupee in the bathroom! Buddy Toupee in the foyer! (*Stops abruptly.*) I'm sorry, there's no one here by that name.
SAM. Adrian Wasp's personal assistant.
BUDDY. That would be Mr. Barkley. He's on another line. Would you like to hold?
SAM. I'm not that tough.

(*SAM hangs up the phone as BUDDY begins to play.*)

SAM. Then I heard the high-heels in the hallway. And a woman who didn't exist walked back into my office.

(*BUDDY finishes with a flourish as LAURA enters.*)

LAURA. Sam. I've been trying to reach you.
SAM. I'm hard to reach.
LAURA. I've heard from Jennifer. She's all right. She said she couldn't bear to face things, so she ran away. Typical.
SAM. What about the compact?

LAURA. The compact? Oh, of course ... She said she lost it weeks ago. I suppose I over-reacted.

SAM. You're good. Awful good at explaining things. Maybe you can explain what Joe Paisley was doing on Mansion Hill last night.

LAURA. Joe Paisley?

SAM. Or what you were doing at Jenny's penthouse on the night of the murder.

LAURA. I wasn't ...

SAM. I just called Wasp Enterprises. They never heard of Laura Vesper.

LAURA. What?!?

SAM. It was you at the penthouse.

LAURA. No—Carol Indigo!

SAM. I have a witness. She calls herself the Princess. You were seen.

LAURA. The Princess...? You're wrong, Sam.

SAM. Am I?

LAURA. There was a woman called the Princess. We never knew her real name. She used to live there.

SAM. Where? In Wasp Tower?

LAURA. In one of the brownstones behind the old concert hall. She'd lived there all her life.

SAM. Until Wasp tossed her out like yesterday's newspaper.

LAURA. It wasn't like that.

SAM. What was it like?

(BUDDY begins to play.)

LAURA. We tried relocation, but the Princess wouldn't leave. You'd see her. In the bus shelter. Standing on a corner. After a while ... you stop seeing her. You have to. It was a cold night in February. Deadly cold. It wasn't our fault ... Jennifer found her in the morning.

(BUDDY has stopped playing.)

SAM. Found her? She was dead?

LAURA. It was a terrible shock for Jennifer. I'm afraid she blamed her father.

(SAM suddenly grabs Laura by the shoulders.)

SAM. Look, I don't care anymore—who blamed who, or what lies you tell me. I don't know what game you're playing, but that's all right; I'm getting used to not knowing anything. I don't know who you are or who killed Wasp, but that's all right too—it's not my business. I hired on to find Jenny.

LAURA. You're hurting me. *(SAM lets her go.)* I don't believe your services are required any longer, Mr. Galahad.

SAM. I'm going to find her.

LAURA. I'll pay you, of course, if you'll just send me your bill.

SAM. Forget it.

LAURA. Please, I like to pay my debts.

SAM. Some debts can't be paid.

(SAM turns his back on her and looks out the window. LAURA exits.)

SAM. Suddenly the room smelled of stale cigarette smoke and shattered dreams. People were vanishing all around me. First Jenny, then Laura, now the Princess. I was tired. Tired of cutting my fingers on a broken-glass jigsaw puzzle. I checked into a little hotel I know where the desk clerk is blind and you sign your name in invisible ink. I had disappeared. *(BUDDY begins to play eerie piano scales.)* It all came down to who killed Adrian Wasp. Was it Jenny? But what about Laura Vesper? Who was she anyway? And then there was the Princess. She was supposed to be dead. And, by the way, just who the hell was Carol Indigo? (*To Buddy.*) You know, you're not being very helpful all of a sudden.

BUDDY. Leave me alone, I'm practicing.

SAM. It was raining again—hard and steady—like that was all it took to wash away the dirt. I looked out the window at the rain—but all I saw was Jenny.

BUDDY. A man named Galahad looked out a window and remembered a time before his world turned gray. A time of bright colors and sharp contrasts. So sharp you could cut yourself.

(*BUDDY plays as the LIGHTS change. We're in the Red Eye Lounge, ten years ago. The blonde is there, listening at the piano. This is JENNY.*)

[Music Cue #16: BEFORE JENNY]

SAM. Pretty song.

JENNY. Nobody plays it like Buddy.

SAM. My name's Sam.

JENNY. I'm Jenny.

(*BUDDY sings as SAM moves to JENNY and THEY begin to dance.*)

BUDDY.
A GLANCE ACROSS A SMOKY BAR
A LOOK, A DANCE, AND THERE YOU ARE
WITH JENNY

SAM. (*As they dance.*) Tell me who you are, and what you're going to be tomorrow, and who you were yesterday.

JENNY. Why? Am I the mysterious type?

SAM. You're no type at all. You're all alone. As indefinable as music.

(*SAM and JENNY move to the piano as BUDDY sings.*)

BUDDY.
IT SEEMS TO ME THAT ONCE YOU'VE MET HER
LIKE A DREAM YOU WON'T FORGET HER
JENNY

JENNY. What are you doing here, Sam? In a bar out by an airport?

SAM. Just looking, I guess. I like it here.

JENNY. Looking? At what?

SAM. I watch the faces come and go. Gives me the illusion I'm going somewhere.

JENNY. Don't you ever want to go along?

SAM. Not 'til now.

(THEY kiss, tentatively at first, then passionately. BUDDY is watching.)

JENNY. (*Suddenly.*) Come with me, Sam. Now. Tonight. Don't ask any questions. Don't say anything.

SAM. The red-eye leaves in an hour. By morning we could be anywhere we want to be.

JENNY. (*Turning away.*) I don't want to talk about the morning.

SAM. Jenny...?

JENNY. (*Starting to cry.*) Why can't tonight go on forever?

SAM. What's all this?

JENNY. Nothing. Just a sad stranger in a bar.

SAM. Maybe we're moving a little too fast. We've got an hour. A couple more drinks. Couple of songs ... (*BUDDY begins to play again.*) I don't even know your last name.

JENNY. (*Changing the subject.*) Get me that drink, will you Sam?

SAM. Sure, I could use one myself. Don't go away.

(SAM exits. JENNY takes a compact from her bag and fixes her face. BUDDY looks at her a moment, then stops playing.)

BUDDY. You're not going to be here when he gets back, are you?

JENNY. Excuse me?

BUDDY. Sorry.

(HE starts to play again. JENNY puts the compact in her bag and takes out an airline ticket.)

JENNY. You know what I'm doing here? I'm running away from home. Like a child. And for a moment—when we were dancing—I could almost see a way out. But it was a dream. My father is expecting me. He doesn't like to be disappointed. *(JENNY closes her bag and turns to go.)*

BUDDY. You forgot your ticket.

JENNY. I can't use it. Give it to Sam

BUDDY. He'll be looking for you.

JENNY. Tell him ... Tell him it's time to stop looking. *(JENNY leaves.)*

BUDDY. I don't think he'll believe me.

(BUDDY plays as the LIGHTS change. The flashback is over. SAM is back at the window.[Music Cue #16A: INTRO TO JENNY])

SAM. I saw her once. Two strangers in a bar by an airport. With a piano in the background. I saw her once. Ten years ago. And I've seen her every moment since.

[Music Cue #17: JENNY]

(Singing.)
OH YES, I'VE SEEN JENNY
PASSING IN STREETCARS
SITTING IN CAFES
OH YES, I'VE SEEN JENNY
WANDERING IN GALLERIES

WEEPING AT MATINEES

JENNY
IN PROFILE, IN SILHOUETTE
IN COLOR, IN BLACK AND WHITE
A FACE FROM SOME PLACE
YOU SUDDENLY REMEMBER
IN THE MIDDLE OF THE NIGHT

SHE WALKS IN MY SLEEP
ON THE EDGES OF WAKING ME
JUST OUT OF REACH
OH, WHERE ARE YOU TAKING ME?
JENNY

OH YES, I'VE SEEN JENNY
SEDUCTIVE AS SHADOWS
ELUSIVE AS LIGHT
OH YES, I'VE SEEN JENNY
LIKE FIREWORKS AT NOON
LIKE A RAINBOW AT NIGHT

JENNY
THROUGH MORNINGS AND AFTERNOONS
THROUGH EVENINGS FROM MIDNIGHT TILL
  DAWN
YOU SEEM IN A DREAM
TO FINALLY HOLD HER IN YOUR ARMS
THEN SUDDENLY SHE'S GONE

ALONE AS THE DAY BREAKS
AND LOST IN CONFUSION
WAS SHE SOMEONE YOU LOVED?
WAS SHE JUST AN ILLUSION?
JENNY

ONLY JENNY EVERYWHERE
HER WALK, HER SMILE, HER SHADE OF HAIR

JENNY SHATTERED LIKE A GLASS
ALIVE IN ALL THE GIRLS THAT PASS
IF ONLY SHE WERE ONE OF THEM
INSTEAD OF ALL AND NONE OF THEM
I'D FIND HER AND FORGET HER
I'D FIND HER AND NOT LET HER
GO ON HAUNTING AND OBSESSING
UTTERLY POSSESSING ME
JENNY
JENNY
JENNY
JENNY

(The LIGHTS fade to BLACK, then come back up as BUDDY plays. LAURA VESPER crosses the stage.)

[Music Cue #18: DON'T KNOW WHAT
I EXPECTED (Reprise)]

BUDDY.
SHE'S A PALE BLONDE WITH RICE PAPER SKIN
HER CHEEKBONES ARE HIGH AND HER LIPS
   ARE THIN
SLIPPIN' IN AND OUT OF DARKNESS LIKE A
   DEJA VU
IN JUST ANOTHER SHADE OF GUNMETAL BLUE

(LIGHTS up on SAM. HE is putting on a shoulder holster.)

SAM. I spotted the tail as I was leaving the Hall of Records. Jenny's paperwork had checked out. Next stop—City Morgue. And Laura Vesper was my shadow.
SAM/BUDDY.
IT'S JUST AS I SUSPECTED
GOT TROUBLE HERE FOR SURE

BUDDY.
THE DETECTIVE
  SAM.
THE DETECTED
  BOTH.
WHEN DID THE LINES BEGIN TO BLUR?
  SAM. The attendant at the Morgue owed me a favor.
She let me peek through the back-log of Jane Does. From
the window I could see the Princess coming town the
street. She made pretty good time—for a dead woman.

(PRINCESS crosses the stage as BUDDY sings.)

  BUDDY.
SHE'S THE CURB-SIDE QUEEN OF DOWN-AND-
  OUT
THE RAGGED RULER IN A KINGDOM OF DOUBT
IS SHE SOMEONE YOU SHOULD KNOW, OR
  RECOGNIZE?
YOU'VE BEEN STARIN' AT HER FEET
'CAUSE IT'S HARD TO MEET HER EYES
  SAM. I stopped by a bar, but I didn't buy a drink. I
bought five dollars worth of quarters and parked myself
in a phone booth. I called every music store in town.
They all gave me the answer I knew I'd get. I was a
detective again. Three cheers for Galahad. Then I did a
little shadowing of my own. I followed the Princess to
Wasp Tower. I didn't follow her inside. I leaned against a
lamppost and waited. I knew who I was going to see.
  BUDDY.
SHE'S A PALE BLONDE
  SAM.
WITH RICE PAPER SKIN
  BUDDY.
WHERE'S SHE GOING?
  SAM.
WHERE'S SHE BEEN?

BUDDY.
NOWHERE
SAM.
EVERYWHERE
BUDDY.
SHE LED YOU QUITE A CHASE
SAM.
THE LAST PIECE OF A PUZZLE, FALLING INTO
PLACE

(CAROL enters.)

SAM. Carol Indigo. I watched her check her make-up
in the light from the streetlamp. In her hand, a compact—
white gold with a single diamond inset.
SAM/CAROL/BUDDY.
IT'S JUST AS I SUSPECTED
GOT TROUBLE HERE FOR SURE
THE DETECTIVE, THE DETECTED
WHEN DID THE LINES BEGIN TO BLUR?
CAROL. Taxi!

*(The LIGHTS BLACKOUT except for a SPOTLIGHT
on BUDDY. HE plays a bass octave tremelo. We are
back in the Red Eye Lounge.)*

BUDDY. Ladies and gentlemen ... Once again, the
Red Eye Lounge is proud to present ... the one ... the
only ... the tipsy ... Miss Carol Indigo!

*(The SPOTLIGHT swings over to CAROL. She's had
more than a few.)*

CAROL. Hit it!

[Music Cue #19: PUT IT ON MY TAB]

LET'S MAKE IT A NIGHT TO REMEMBER

A NIGHT OF CHAMPAGNE AND CAVIAR
DON'T MISUNDERSTAND
I GOT NO CASH ON HAND
BUT I RUN A TAB AT THIS BAR
SO ORDER ANYTHING YOU WANT
ANYTHING YOUR HEART DESIRES
WHEN IT'S HOT WHY NOT
FAN THE FIRES?
THE NIGHT'S A PUP, SO BOTTOMS UP
THEY'LL HAVE TO POUR US INTO A CAB
FORGET THE BILL
DON'T WORRY, WE'LL
PUT IT ON MY TAB

(Picking someone out in the audience.)

Hey, mister ... Hey, mister! How'd you like to buy a girl a drink? I could use one. I drink to forget. And then ... I forget to drink.

(SAM enters the Red Eye Lounge. HE watches Carol.)

CAROL.
I'M A PINK LADY
IN A GOLDEN CADILLAC
I LIKE MY MARYS BLOODY
AND MY RUSSIANS BLACK
JACK DANIELS, JOHNNY WALKER
THOSE BOYS HAVE MET THEIR MATCH
JUST LINE 'EM UP
AND IT'S DOWN THE HATCH

TOMORROW WE CAN WORRY 'BOUT THE WHY
  AND HOW
BUT NOW I'LL JUST TAKE WHAT I CAN GRAB
AND WHAT THE HELL
WE MIGHT AS WELL
PUT IT ON MY TAB

YES, WE'LL HAVE A NIGHT TO REMEMBER
A NIGHT OF NIGHT-AFTER-NIGHTS
OUR CREDIT EXTENDS
BUT YOU KNOW HOW IT ENDS
THEY'LL PULL OUT THE PHONE
AND THEY'LL TURN OUT THE LIGHTS
BUT I'LL REST IN PEACE, MY THRIFTY FRIEND
I WON'T BE TWISTING IN MY GRAVE
OVER DOUGH I WOULDN'T SPEND
AND COULDN'T SAVE
I WON'T TRY TO WHEEDLE
THROUGH THE EYE OF A NEEDLE
WHEN I'M JUST A BODY ON A SLAB
YOU MAY LAUGH BUT MY EPITAPH'LL BE
"PUT IT ON HER ...
PUT IT ON HER ...
PUT IT ON HER ...
... TAB"

*(After her number, CAROL sits at a table with a drink.
SAM crosses to her as BUDDY plays cocktail
MUSIC. [Music Cue #19A: COCKTAIL MUSIC II]*

SAM. Miss Indigo?
CAROL. Who wants to know?
SAM. Just a fan. I enjoyed your singing.
CAROL. Disappear.
SAM. I tried it once. I kept having flashbacks.
CAROL. You should drink more. I drink to forget.
SAM. Does it work?
CAROL. What?
SAM. Forget it.
CAROL. Say, you're cute. What do you drink?
SAM. Bourbon, usually.
CAROL. Bourbon. I thought so. Nothing but
trouble.

SAM. Trouble's my middle name. It used to be Tall-Dark-and-Handsome, but I changed it.

CAROL. You're funny. I like you.

SAM. (*Taking out cassette tape.*) I have something that belongs to you. I thought you might want it back.

CAROL. Belongs...? To me...?

SAM. I got it from a friend of yours—Adrian Wasp.

CAROL. Daddy-O? How's he doing?

SAM. Daddy-O's feeling no pain.

CAROL. Like me.

SAM. When did you see him last?

CAROL. I forget. Couple of nights ago.

SAM. Where?

CAROL. Mansion Hill. Daddy-O was depressed. Real down, you know?

SAM. What about?

CAROL. Jennifer, of course. It's always about Jennifer.

SAM. You look like a lady who can take a man's mind off his troubles.

CAROL. Daddy-O says I'm beautiful. We had a little party.

SAM. Just the two of you?

CAROL. Say—what do you think I am? It was a party. Me and Daddy-O, and Miss Vesper ... little party-pooper. She told me to take my music and get out.

SAM. So there was music?

CAROL. The tape. Somebody put on the tape. And I danced. Danced with Daddy-O. But he'd had a little too much to drink. Let's us dance, Bourbon, you and me.

SAM. Later. I want you to sing.

CAROL. (*To Buddy.*) Hit it!

SAM. Hang on, Buddy. (*To Carol.*) About the night of the murder.

CAROL. Now who's a party-pooper?

SAM. Knock off the baby talk.

CAROL. You're not so cute anymore.

SAM. What happened that night?

CAROL. Dancing with Daddy-O.
SAM. What broke up the dancing?
CAROL. He said I was beautiful.
SAM. What else did he say?
CAROL. I want a drink!
SAM. To forget what?

(CAROL turns into Laura.)

LAURA. Sam. I've been trying to reach you.
SAM. Hello, Laura.
LAURA. I've heard from Jennifer. She's all right. She said she couldn't bear ...
SAM. I know, you told me. We've already played that scene. I want to talk about the paperwork.
LAURA. Paperwork?
SAM. The paperwork Jenny had put together. The evidence against Wasp. *(SAM holds up envelope.)*
LAURA. *(Reaching for the envelope.)* Give it to me!!
SAM. That's the real reason you hired me.
LAURA. Lies!
SAM. You'd do anything to protect the family.
LAURA. Jennifer's lies!!
SAM. Anything to cover-up the truth about Wasp.

(LAURA grabs the envelope and turns into the PRINCESS.)

PRINCESS. Sam! You got it solved yet?
SAM. I'm working on it, Princess.
PRINCESS. *(Handing envelope back.)* Keep it, Sam. I think it's a clue.
SAM. You were the key to the whole case. The reason Jenny took such a sudden interest in her father's business.
PRINCESS. I thought you were supposed to be a detective. Jenny never knew I was alive.
SAM. Maybe not. But she knew you were dead.

PRINCESS. ... dead?

SAM. Jenny was the one who found you. Frozen to death in a bus shelter. That was when she started going through the old files, asking questions. She went to Mansion Hill. She confronted Wasp with the evidence.

CAROL. Let's dance, Bourbon.

SAM. But Jenny is very fragile—like glass ...

(The BLONDE'S various personalities begin to emerge in rapid succession.)

LAURA. Jennifer is unstable.

SAM. It doesn't take much pressure to crack the glass.

PRINCESS. I never seen her.

SAM. It isn't easy to see in the hot, white light that allows no shadow. That's how Jenny saw her father.

CAROL. Too close ... Dancing too close ...

SAM. And the crack in the glass was a spider's web. A gun appeared—cold and blue ...

PRINCESS. Cold ... I'm so cold ...

SAM. I don't think she even heard the gunshot, only the sound of breaking glass. The compact hit the hardwood floor, something shattered ... and Jenny disappeared.

LAURA. Forever, Mr. Galahad. Gone where you can't find her. Jennifer killed her father. (*LAURA kisses Sam hard on the mouth. Then SHE slaps his face.*) It's over, Sam.

(LAURA crosses to exit. SAM yells after her.)

SAM. Jenny!

(LAURA stops. CAROL turns around.)

CAROL. Let her go, Bourbon. She's better off lost.

(CAROL looks around. She's forgotten that Laura wanted to make an exit, so SHE crosses to her table and sits with her drink. SAM stands alone. BUDDY begins to play.)

[Music Cue #19B: UNDERSCORING]

BUDDY. Sorry, Sam.

SAM. So am I, Buddy. We're all pretty sorry.

BUDDY. What do you mean?

SAM. Jenny didn't kill Wasp. You did.

CAROL. Him???!!!

BUDDY. Sam—I'm just the piano player.

SAM. Wasp was on his way to the airport on the night of the murder. It was here, in the Red Eye Lounge, that Jenny caught up with him. They went to Mansion Hill, and you followed them. You went around to the back of the house. You peeked in the window.

BUDDY. You're talking crazy.

SAM. You had a gun. You forced your way in. You were after the evidence—so you could ruin Wasp's life the way he ruined yours.

BUDDY. What do I care about Wasp?

SAM. You hated Wasp for tearing down the old Metro Concert Hall.

BUDDY. No.

SAM. And tearing down your crazy dream.

BUDDY. No!!

SAM. Buddy Toupee—The Virtuoso.

BUDDY. You got nothing on me.

SAM. *(Taking out the tape.)* Only this. "Buddy Toupee—Live!" It's not available in stores. But I got one. I got it from the Princess. The Princess got it from Carol. She got it from Laura, who got it from Jenny, who got it from you—on the night of the murder. You put on the tape. You made Wasp listen. And then it all went to hell.

(BUDDY reaches into his inside coat pocket. SAM pulls his gun.)

SAM. Start playing, Buddy. I'd kind of like to keep track of your hands right now.

(BUDDY slowly removes his hand from his pocket. It holds a handkerchief. HE wipes his brow.)

BUDDY. Any requests?
CAROL. Play the one you played for Daddy-O.
BUDDY. No! Not that!!
SAM. Go on, Buddy.
BUDDY. Please, Sam ...
SAM. You played it for Wasp, you can play it for her.
BUDDY. For her?
SAM. Play it!
BUDDY. *(Begins to play.)* [Music Cue #20: THE VIRTUOSO] Of all the cocktail lounges in all the world, Adrian Wasp had to walk into mine.
YOU THINK THIS WAS MY DREAM
THE PLACE THAT I WANTED TO BE
YOU THINK THAT I SAT AND PRACTICED FOR YEARS
TO SIT AND PLAY MUSIC THAT NOBODY HEARS
WELL, THIS WASN'T MY DREAM AT ALL
WHEN I DREAMED,
I DREAMED OF THAT ONE CONCERT HALL

WHERE THE CURTAIN WOULD RISE
ON THOUSANDS OF EYES
EAGERLY AWAITING
CHANDELIERS WOULD DIM
EVERY HEART WOULD BRIM
THEY'RE ANTICIPATING
THE DELIGHT OF
THE FIRST SIGHT OF

THE VIRTUOSO
OH, SO FULL OF BEAUTY AND TRUTH
THE VIRTUOSO
OH, SO FULL OF PASSION AND YOUTH

NOW I DON'T PLAY BARTOK
I HEAR BAR TALK
THROUGH EVERYTHING I PLAY
NOW INSTEAD OF CHOPIN
I'M PLAYIN' SHOW TUNES
ALL NIGHT AND DAY

ONCE I WAS MAN ENOUGH
FOR RACHMANINOFF
I'D HANDLE HANDEL
WITH THE BEST
NOW IT'S EASY LISTENIN'
AND GOLDEN OLDIES
AND BUDDY, HEY BUDDY,
COULD YOU TAKE A REQUEST

THE VIRTUOSO
OH, SO FULL OF BEAUTY AND TRUTH
THE VIRTUOSO
OH, SO FULL OF PASSION AND YOUTH
A WORLD OF MUSIC, JOY AND LOVE
WAS WAITING,
WAITING LIKE A DREAM TO COME TRUE
… DREAM TO COME …
… MY DREAM …

(BUDDY stops for a moment. The BLONDE is staring at him. SHE starts to cross to the piano as BUDDY continues. SAM watches them.)

BUDDY.
BUT WHEN I LOST MY PLACE TO PLAY
I LET THE MUSIC SLIP AWAY

THROUGH MY FINGERS, DAY BY DAY
'TIL THERE WAS NOTHING LEFT ...

    JENNY. I thought I killed him. My God ... I thought
I killed him.

*(SHE and BUDDY share a look. HE shakes his head
slightly and continues to play. JENNY takes out the
compact, trying to see her reflection in the shattered
mirror. SAM crosses to behind her.)*

    SAM. My name's Sam.

*(JENNY lifts her eyes from the mirror. SHE looks
straight ahead.)*

    JENNY. I'm ... Jenny.

*(SAM touches her. He's finally found her. The MUSIC
finishes. There is silence.)*

    JENNY. Is it over?
    SAM. It's all solved.

*(Their eyes have yet to meet. Now that it's over, they
don't know how to begin. BUDDY starts to play the
melancholy tune from the top of the show. SAM
crosses to the piano. JENNY watches him. BUDDY
stops playing. HE looks at Sam. SAM takes out the
tape.)*

    SAM. The cops may never connect you with this, but
it might be an idea if you went on the road for a while.

*(SAM places the tape in Buddy's "tips" glass. JENNY is
watching him. THEIR eyes meet. SHE smiles.)*

    BUDDY. Thanks, Sam.

(BUDDY begins to play. The LIGHTS seem different—
warmer, somehow. It is morning.)

JENNY. It's been night for so long, and I've been so afraid. Now here it is morning and I'm scared to death.

SAM. Only children are afraid of the dark. When you grow up you understand, it's the mornings you gotta watch out for.

[Music Cue #21: FINALE ACT TWO]

BUDDY.
BRING ME BACK MY CHILDHOOD DAYS
THE SKY WHEN IT WAS BLUE
RAIN WHEN IT WAS PURE
AND LOVE WHEN IT WAS TRUE

JENNY. Ten years ago. That girl. She was just one part of me. A fragment. I'm not your dream, Sam.

SAM. Jenny, all my life I've done nothing but dream. It's a seductive pastime. Mysterious. After a while, you fall in love with the mystery. If you solve it, what have you got?

JENNY. I'll show you mystery.
THE MYSTERY OF MORNING LIGHT
OF EVERY DAY AND EVERY NIGHT
THE MYSTERY OF LETTING GO
WHILE HOLDING TIGHT

SAM/JENNY.
GIVE ME BACK YOUR HEART AGAIN
I'LL NEVER LET IT GO
CAN THE STORY START AGAIN?
CAN YOU SEE I LOVE YOU SO?

(SAM and JENNY kiss as BUDDY plays. Then, as HE
sings, THEY gather at the piano.)

BUDDY.
TAKE THE MOMENT, FIND THE TIME

NOW—BEFORE IT DISAPPEARS
   JENNY.
TIME WILL HEAL THE LOSS
   SAM.
LOVE WILL HEAL THE PAIN
   SAM/JENNY/BUDDY.
IN THE MORNING LIGHT
WE CAN FIND OUR LIVES AGAIN

(BUDDY plays as JENNY picks up the envelope. SHE and SAM walk toward the exit. The LIGHTS start to fade. BUDDY turns to the audience.)

   BUDDY.
BON VOYAGE, MON VOYEUR
ISN'T PEEPING A SIN?
BUT IT'S SO HARD TO STOP IT
ONCE YOU BEGIN
SO HARD TO STEP BACK
FROM THE DREAM, THE MIRAGE
LET BUDDY DRAW THE CURTAIN
(Spoken.) Mon voyeur ...
BON VOYAGE

(The LIGHT fades on BUDDY. BLACKOUT.)

END OF PLAY